POCKET
HEROES

# FLORENCE
# NIGHTINGIRL

## DAVE WOODS
## CHRIS INNS

ORCHARD

Florence Nightingale was famously
known as 'The Lady of the Lamp'.
She was a nurse in tough times. But
when she was little, she was the nurse in
nursery rhymes!

She was Florence Nightingirl!

ONCE UPON A TIME…in the Land of Fairy Tales, something was wrong. The stories had lost their Happily Ever After!

On this day, a large crowd of fairy-tale characters had gathered outside the Town Library. (It had multi-story parking.)

And, these characters weren't happily ever after, either. (Not a bit.)

Dragons were fuming.

Damsels were distressed.

A giant was hugely disappointed.

Little Miss Muffet was a little bit miffed.

A handsome prince was in an ugly mood.

A group of dwarves were getting very short-tempered.

A troll had...well, you get the idea.

Yes, things were going from bad to worse.

(Then back to bad again.)

But then, on this dark day (so the story goes) came a bright spark. A little sprite that carried a light. A young lady with a will of iron, a heart of steel and the clothes of, er…a nurse.

It was Florence Nightingirl!

"IS THERE A PROBLEM HERE?" demanded the tiny nurse.

"There's been a
GRIMEWAVE!" said Dick
Whittington, the Mayor of
London.

"Has there indeed?"
remarked Florence
Nightingirl.

"Yes, things have got GRIMIER and
GRIMIER!" added Puss, to boot.

"Where exactly?" she enquired.

"ALL OVER THE LAND OF FAIRY TALES!" blubbed a little boy (who was feeling blue).

"Hmm…" said Florence Nightingirl. "Tell me more…"

"THE CHILDREN'S STORIES ARE ALL MUCKY!" cried Little Riding Hood (whose face was red with anger).

"Go on…" encouraged the tiny nurse, with great patience.

The farmer's wife (who'd never seen such a thing in her life) said:

"THE STORIES ARE SHODDY, THE TALES ARE TATTY, THE LEGENDS ARE LOUSY, THE RHYMES ARE A CRIME, AND THE VERSE IS WORSE… SOMEBODY NEEDS TO CLEAN UP THIS TOWN!"

Florence Nightingirl nodded knowingly. "IN SHORT…" said the even shorter nurse, "STORYLAND…" and she held up her little nightlight so it shone like a beacon, "…IS UNHYGIENIC!" She checked her nurse's watch. "It's time to organise a team…that are lean…and mean…and provide a sheen…wherever they've been!"

(And with that, she made a clean exit…)

SPIC & SPAN →

"The twins here will clean up any bad English…at the double!"

← GRUNGE

"He's really tough on grime – in fact, he's built up quite a collection of litterbugs."

"Got dirt in your i? Want to clean up your A, C and T? Then Splashy's your man (well, machine)."

SUCKY THE VACUUM CLEANER

"Don't mess with this clean machine or you won't see him for dust. In fact he'll show you a clean pair of wheels."

So Florence Nightingirl and the National Elf Service set off on their quest to clean up Storyland…one page at a time.

In the first fairy tale they wandered into, they came upon a tower.

*And high in the tower…*
*someone with girl power…*
*was playing pop hits*
*(and squeezing her zits).*

"Rapunzel, Rapunzel, let down your hair," cried Florence Nightingirl.

Rapunzel's big hair came tumbling down in a big way. The little nurse gave it a big examination.

"I thought so," said Florence Nightingirl. "NITS!"

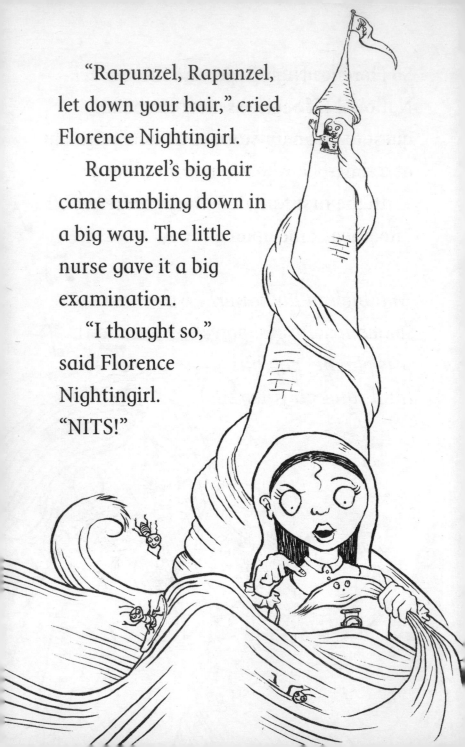

"Bad hair day!" mumbled Rapunzel.

"Not for long!" said Florence. The National Elf Service took Rapunzel straight to the barber, who, to cut a long story short…and long hair even shorter…cut off all her hair! (So, in days of old it wasn't just knights who were bald.)

"Rapunzel, Rapunzel, we got rid of your hair…" said Florence Nightingirl.

"IT'S UNHYGIENIC!"

Florence Nightingirl's journey took her
and the National Elf Service deep into
one particularly dusty old nursery rhyme.
There, they found…

*Little Miss Muffet, sat on a tuffet,*
*Eating her curds and whey.*
*Along came a spider…*

…who was immediately
caught in an empty jam jar
by Florence Nightingirl
(she'd spied 'er spider).

"Wh-wh-why am I so afraid?" said Little Miss Muffet.

Who had, indeed, almost been frightened away.

"You've got…" said Florence Nightingirl, "arachnophobia!"

(That's a scarily long word for being scared of spiders.)

"What can I do?" cried Little Miss Muffet.

Florence Nightingirl handed Little Miss Muffet an Ugly-Duckling-Feather-Duster and said, "Well, you can start by getting rid of all those cobwebs…

THEY'RE UNHYGIENIC!"

Florence Nightingirl and the National
Elf Service travelled across more famous
old stories until they heard music
coming from a nearby field.
They peeked over the fence and heard:

*Hey diddle diddle, the cat and the*
*fiddle, the cow jumped over the moon.*
*The little dog laughed, to see such fun,*
*and the dish ran away with the spoo—*

"NOT SO FAST!" shouted Florence Nightingirl.

The National Elf Service leapt into action. Soapy and Squeaky quickly put the dish and the spoon into Splashy the Dishwasher. (On a hot wash.)

"Well..." said Florence Nightingirl, "THEY'RE UNHYGIENIC!"

Florence Nightingirl could hear bleating coming from the neighbouring field. She and the National Elf Service peered around the hedgerow…

*Mary had a little lamb,*
*Its fleece was white as snow.*
*And everywhere that Mary went—*

"TICKS AND LICE ARE SURE TO GO!" barked Florence. "PREPARE THE SHEEP-DIP! And while you're there, team," added Florence Nightingirl, "give Mary a dip, too…

SHE'S UNHYGIENIC!"

After travelling through a few more
nursery rhymes, Florence Nightingirl
and the National Elf Service came upon
a high wall. At the bottom of the wall,
lots of horses and men were fussing
around a large, egg-shaped gentleman
– who looked a bit…well, scrambled.

"RIGHT!" said
Florence Nightingirl,
"I'm calling ELF
AND SAFETY!

This isn't acceptable. Humpty should have been wearing a crash helmet, there were no handholds and he should've been accompanied by a parent or guardian..."

Florence Nightingirl beckoned over the National Elf Service. "Clean this mess up, team," she said. "IT'S UNHYGIENIC!"

(They took Humpty Dumpty to be eggs-rayed, but it was nothing more than a cracking headache. Oh, and a bit of shell-shock.)

When they came back, they found:

*Two little dicky birds sitting on the wall,*
*One named Peter, one named Paul,*
*Fly away, Peter, fly away, Pau—*

"LOOK AT ALL THOSE BIRD
DROPPINGS!" cried Florence Nightingirl.

She turned to the National Elf Service
again. "Scrubby! Get the Scarecrow
from The Wizard of Oz over here to keep
these birds away. THEY'RE VERY, VERY
UNHYGIENIC!"

Florence Nightingirl and the National Elf
Service took a path that led into a deep,
dark wood. Along the forest path she
met two little children. It was Hansel and
Gretel.

Both gave Florence Nightingirl a big,
beaming smile.

"Hang on…" said Florence. "Let me
have a closer look at those teeth…"

Florence peered into their mouths.

"Just as I expected!" she tutted. "Most children have a sweet tooth – but you two children have whole sets of sweet teeth! I'll make you an appointment to see the Tooth Fairy—"

"For what time?" asked Hansel and Gretel.

"Tooth-hurty," grinned Florence Nightingirl.

The sweet children began to sidle off – with sour looks.

"One more thing," shouted Florence Nightingirl. "Stay away from the witch's sweet cottage...IT'S UNHYGIENIC!"

Florence Nightingirl and the National Elf Service travelled far beyond the forest until they came upon a castle. In the castle lived a very happy monarch…

*Old King Cole was a merry old soul,*
*and a merry old soul was he.*
*He called for his pipe and he—*

"OI! NO SMOKING
– THIS IS A
CHILDREN'S
BOOK!" pointed
out Florence
Nightingirl.
She whipped
the pipe out
of Old King
Cole's mouth and
handed it to Scoury.

Oi!

"Dispose of that,"
she ordered.
"IT'S UNHYGIENIC!"

But now:

*Old King Cole wasn't a merry old soul,
and a merry old soul wasn't he...
So Florence Nightingirl, who'd hidden
his pipe, called for his fiddlers three.*

Well, she thought it might cheer him
up a bit.

(And it certainly stopped him
fuming.)

Suddenly, Florence Nightingirl heard a kerfuffle from the pantry:

*Georgie Porgie, pudding and pie,*
*Kissed the girls and made them cry...*

"STOP THAT IMMEDIATELY!" said Florence Nightingirl. "KISSING IS UNHYGIENIC!"
She then glanced at her nurse's watch.
"Hmmm..." she said, thoughtfully. "Almost one o'clock."

*Hickory dickory dock,*
*The mouse ran up the clock.*
*The clock struck one,*
*The mouse ran down...*

And was immediately caught in a humane trap by one of the National Elf Service.

"Rodent infestation!" remarked Florence Nightingirl. "VERY UNHYGIENIC!"

Florence Nightingirl and the National Elf Service continued to travel far and wide. Towards dinnertime, they arrived at a cottage owned by a man named Jack:

*Jack Sprat could eat no fat,*
*his wife could eat no lean...*

"YOU TWO NEED A BETTER NUTRITIONAL DIET!" Florence Nightingirl informed them.

She noticed that Jack Sprat and his wife were licking their lips.

(Of course, they'd rather have been licking the plate.)

"And if you think that betwixt you both you'll lick that platter clean, you've got another thing coming... IT'S UNHYGIENIC!"

Soapy stuck the plate in Splashy the Dishwasher.

Meanwhile, Florence Nightingirl examined the rest of the kitchen.

She found…

*Little Jack Horner sat in the corner, eating his Christmas pie.*
*He put in his thumb and pulled out a plum, and said, "What a good boy am I!"*

"ER, DID YOU WASH YOUR HANDS?" demanded Florence Nightingirl.

Little Jack looked a little embarrassed.

"Not such a good boy then, are you?"
Florence got Spic & Span to wash
Little Jack Horner's thumbs.
And hands.
And wrists.
And forearms.
And elbows.
(Well, you
know what nurses
are like.)

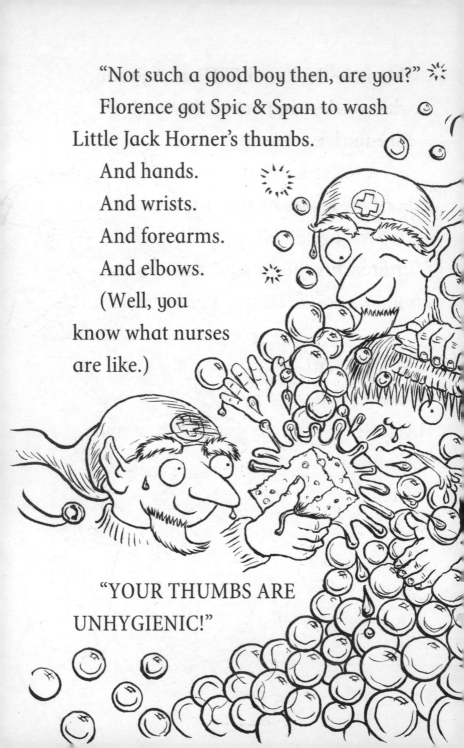

"YOUR THUMBS ARE
UNHYGIENIC!"

"Look, it's Jack and Jill!" cried Grunge, who was looking out of the window through his telescope.

(A telescope he'd borrowed from a certain pirate in Treasure Island.)

*Jack and Jill went up the hill,*
*to fetch a pail of water.*
*Jack fell down and broke his crown...*

…and Florence Nightingirl was there in a jiffy with her first aid kit.

"Scoury, bring me some surgical dressing, please. None of this vinegar and brown paper nonsense!"

"And Jack," said Florence Nightingirl, "get rid of Jill. SHE'S UNHYGIENIC!"

Beyond Jack and Jill's hill, Florence Nightingirl found another series of foothills. And on one of these foothills was…a shoe.

*There was an old woman who lived in a shoe…*

"NOT ACCEPTABLE!" cried Florence Nightingirl. "Spic & Span, find me the world's largest odour-eater, please. Then lay it as carpet in there.

IT'S UNHYGIENIC!"

In the next town that they journeyed through, a large crowd of children had gathered.

*Ring-a-ring o' roses,*
*A pocket full of posies.*
*A-tishoo! A-tishoo!*
*We all fall d—*

"CATCH IT. BIN IT. KILL IT!" exclaimed Florence Nightingirl. And the National Elf Service made Sucky the Vacuum Cleaner suck up all the discarded tissues.

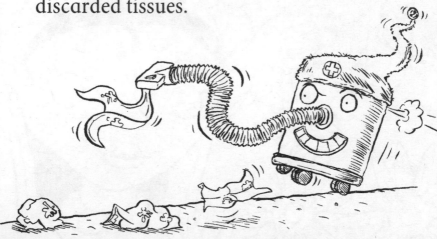

"SNEEZING IS UNHYGIENIC!"

From out of one of the pocket full of posies crawled an insect...

*Ladybird, Ladybird, fly away home,*
*Your house—*

"—has been fitted with a smoke alarm," Florence Nightingirl informed her.

"So your children are safe."

"That's terribly kind of you," said a terribly tired-looking princess who was having terrible trouble sleeping.

In fact, she had bags under her eyes. (Yes sir, yes sir, two bags full, sir.)

"Remake her bed..." said Florence Nightingirl, "without the pea under the mattress!"

She then examined the Three Little Pigs who'd come up in a rash (of bacon) because they were allergic to the wolf hair on their chinny-chin-chins (it made them huff and puff).

"Give them some oinkment," she prescribed.

The Three Little Pigs wolfed it down (and it kept them in the pink).

Then, another little piggy went past: "Wee-wee-wee, all the way home—"

"OH NO YOU DON'T!" cried Florence Nightingirl.

She swept the piglet into her arms
and handed it to Squeaky.

"Get a nappy on him!" she said.

"WEE-WEE-WEEING

EVERYWHERE IS UNHYGIENIC!"

Florence Nightingirl and the National Elf Service's journey had been long and winding. They had worked their way through the Land of Fairy Tales, cleaning up one tale after another. And now…no Fairy Tales were Grimm… the endings had been happily-ever-aftered…

(Even Christian Andersen had washed his Hans…)

But now…poor Florence Nightingirl was as tired as a storyteller's tongue.

She felt like sleeping for a hundred years.

"THEY'RE ALL UNHYGIENIC…" she wailed, feebly. Then she flopped onto a Golden-Goose-Feather-Duvet.

(Oh dear, she was as sick as a Never-Neverland pirate's parrot.)

"I have to continue cleaning up the Land of Fairy Tales," she groaned.

"You can't!" said the National Elf Service.

"Says who?" moaned Florence Nightingirl.

"SAYS YOU!" they said. "LOOK…"
A sign read:

TO WHICHEVER FAIRY-TALE
CHARACTER IT MAY CONCERN:

Anyone who is sick, poorly, ill,
off-colour, peaky, under the weather
or has so much as a sniffle:

## MUST STAY IN BED!

(THIS SIGN IS NOT TO BE SNIFFED AT)

SIGNED:

*Florence Nightingirl.*

FLORENCE NIGHTINGIRL
THE FAIRY-TALE NURSE

"FLORENCE NIGHTINGIRL…"
said the National Elf Service, "under
your own orders, you must stay in bed
because…

YOU'RE UNHYGIENIC!"

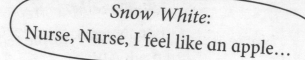

Finally, all the stories ended
HAPPILY EVER AFTER.
(But all the Nurse, Nurse jokes made
the little nurse feel worse, worse!)

And what became of Florence Nightingirl?
Well, that's another story…

FURTHER READING!
RAPUNZEL'S HAIRSTYLES
by Aaron Floor
DODGY ANIMALS
by Barbara Blacksheep
CREATING FAIRYTALES
VOLUME II
by Drew Pictures
CREATING FAIRYTALES
VOLUME I
by Tilda Tale
DANCING IN CASTLES
by Hans Knessanboomsidaisy
HOW TO READ QUICKLY
by Skipper Paige
IMAGINARY CREATURES
by VIC TITIOUS
BUG OFF!

# DAVE WOODS
# CHRIS INNS

| | |
|---|---|
| SHORT JOHN SILVER | 978 1 40831 359 6 |
| SIR LANCE-A-LITTLE | 978 1 40831 360 2 |
| ROBIN HOODIE | 978 1 40831 364 0 |
| JUNIOR CAESAR | 978 1 40831 362 6 |
| FLORENCE NIGHTINGIRL | 978 1 40831 363 3 |
| HENRY THE 1/8$^{\text{TH}}$ | 978 1 40831 361 9 |

All softbacks priced at £4.99

Orchard Books are available from all good bookshops,
or can be ordered from our website: www.orchardbooks.co.uk,
or telephone 01235 827702, or fax 01235 827703.